Rain

Written and illustrated by
Manya Stojic

PAVILION

It was hot.

Everything was hot and dry.

Rain

In memory of my dad, Lyuba, with whom
I enjoyed watching thunderstorms

This edition first published in the United Kingdom in 2015 by

Pavilion Children's Books
1 Gower Street
London, WC1E 6HD

An imprint of Pavilion Books Company Limited

This book is a reissue of *Rain* (Dragonfly Books, 2000)
and was published originally as *Rain* (David Bennet Books, 2000)

This edition copyright © Pavilion Children's Books

The moral rights of the authors have been asserted.

ISBN: 9781843653059

A CIP catalogue record for this book is available from the British Library.

20 19 18 17 16 15
10 9 8 7 6 5 4 3 2 1

Printed by 1010 Printing International Ltd, China
Reproduction by ColourDepth, UK

This book can be ordered direct from the publisher at the website:
www.pavilionbooks.com, or try your local bookshop.

The red soil was hot and dry and cracked.

A porcupine sniffed around.
"It's time," she whispered.
"The rain is coming! I can smell it. I must tell the zebras."

Lightning **flashed.**
" **The rain is coming!** "
said the zebras.

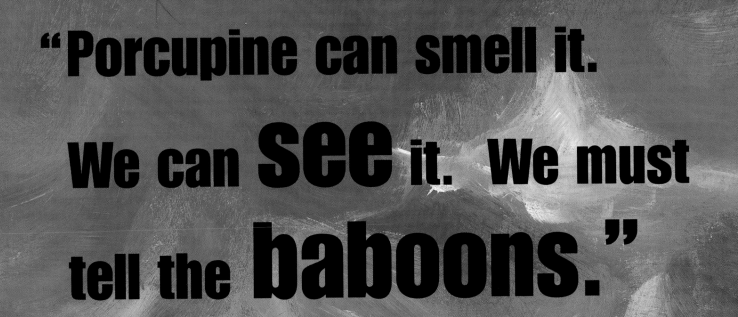

"Porcupine can smell it. We can **see** it. We must tell the **baboons**."

Thunder
boomed.

"**The rain is coming!**"
cried the baboons.

"**Porcupine
can smell it.
The zebras
can see it.
We can hear it.
We must tell
the rhino.**"

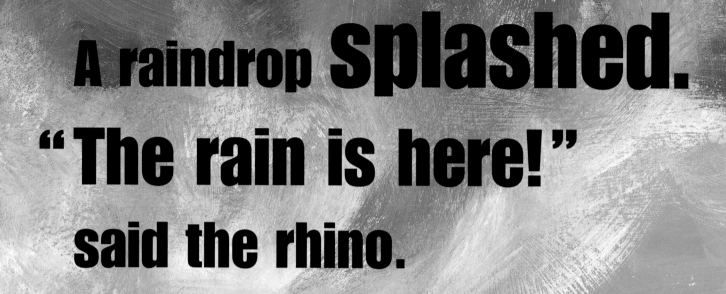

A raindrop **splashed.**
"**The rain is here!**"
said the rhino.

"**Porcupine smelled it.**
The zebras saw it.
The baboons heard it.

And I **felt** it.
I must tell
the **lion.**"

The lion
spoke
in a
deep
purr.

"Yes, the rain is here.

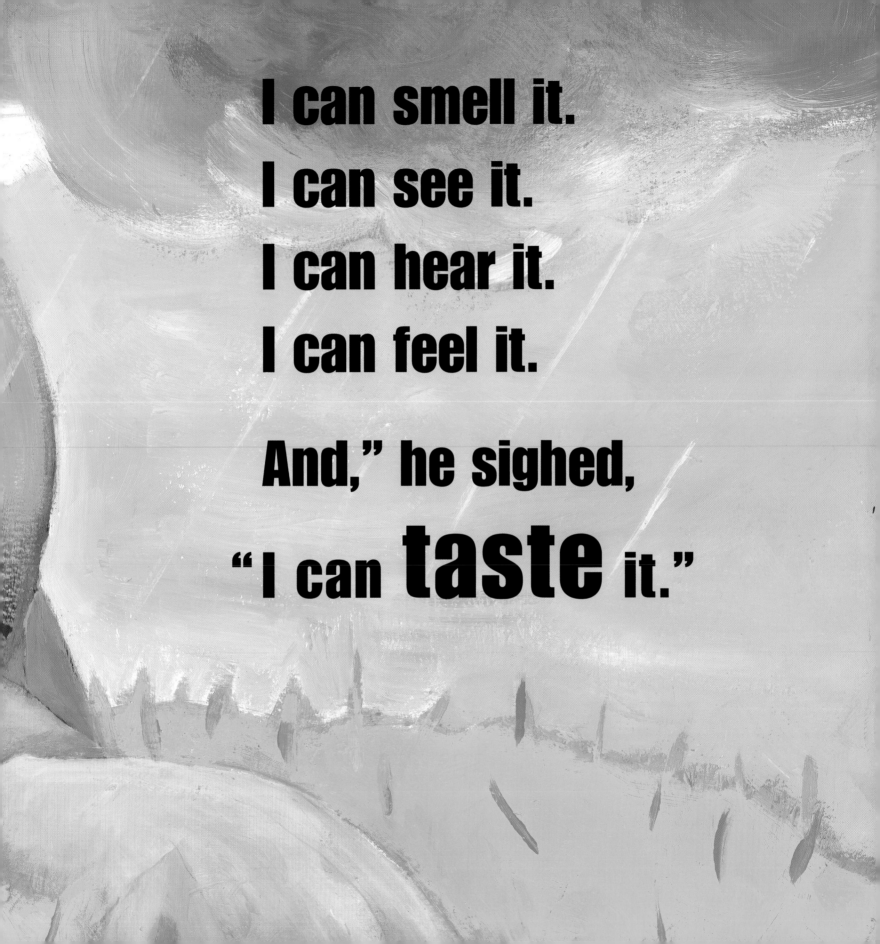

I can smell it.
I can see it.
I can hear it.
I can feel it.

And," he sighed,

"I can **taste** it."

It rained

and it

rained

and it

rained.

It rained until every river **gushed** and **gurgled.**

It rained until every water hole was **full.**

Then the rain stopped and everywhere long, feathery grasses grew from the soil.

Every tree began to sprout fresh, green leaves.

"I can't taste the rain now," purred the lion,

"but I can enjoy the shade of these **big, green leaves.**"

"I can't feel the rain now," said the rhino,

"but I can lie in the cool, soft, squelchy mud."

"We can't hear the rain now," shouted the baboons,

"but we can eat

**fresh,
juicy fruit**
from the trees."

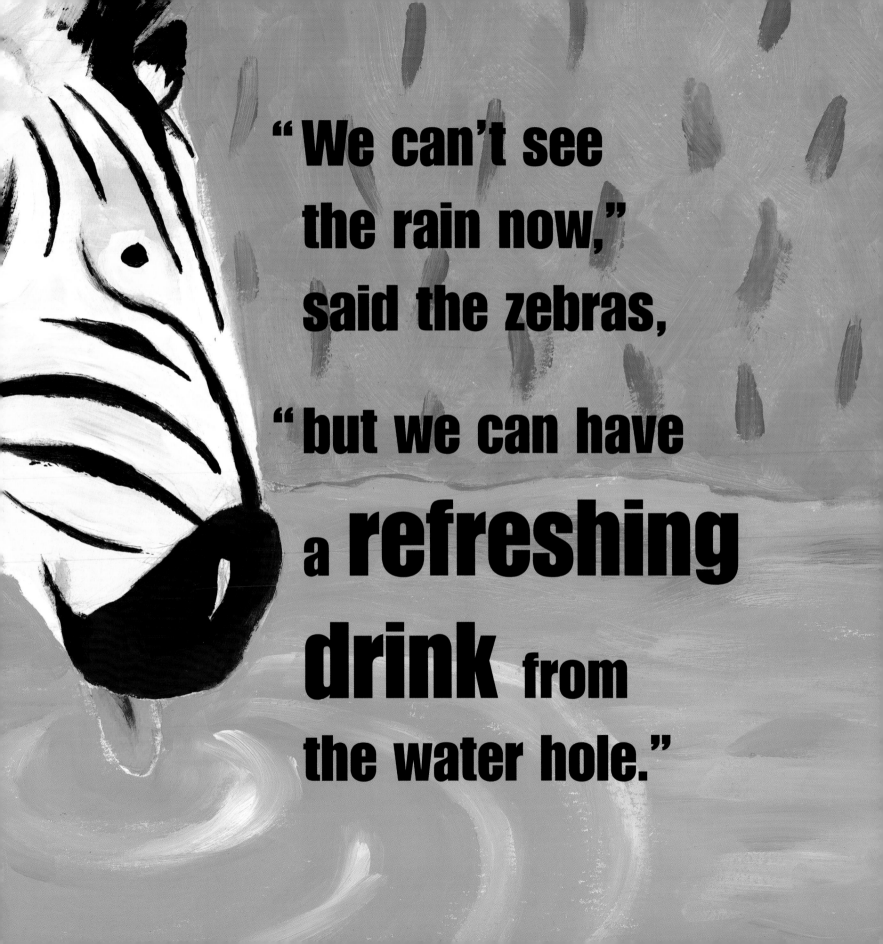

"We can't see the rain now," said the zebras, "but we can have a **refreshing** **drink** from the water hole."

"I can't smell the rain now," whispered the porcupine, "but **I know** that it will come back again. When it's **time.**"

The sun shone over the plain.

It was **hot.** Everything was drying out.

The red soil was
hot and dry.

A tiny crack appeared.